Dasher © 2018

Written by: Joe Bigley
Illustrated by: Rob White II

ISBN #9781986315555

Printed by CreateSpace, An Amazon.com Company
Available from Amazon.com and other online stores

Hi! My name is Dasher.
Welcome to my home:
the North Pole!

You may know that I am one of the eight reindeer who pull Santa's sleigh. I'm mentioned in that song about a famous reindeer Do you remember how it goes?

Sing it with me, "You know Dasher and Dancer and Prancer and..."

Do you know why or how I can fly? I didn't think so!

But that, my friend, is why I'm here. I'll tell you the untold history of the North Pole, Santa and the reindeer

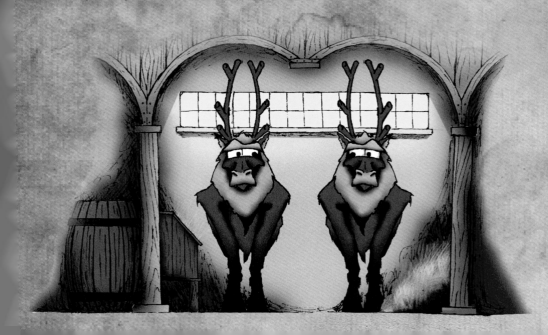

The first thing you should probably know is my birthday. Yes, it is December 24th, but this is not why I'm on Santa's sleigh. There's a lot more to it than that.

My journey began on my second birthday when I saw the front page of our local newspaper

The Polar Press

ISSUE 1224

Attention Young Reindeer

- Do you have unique talents?

- Are you looking for adventure?

- Are you ready to join an elite team?

Do you have what it takes for...

JSN

Trevor Whistler presents:

Proper Brush & Beard Care

The Bible does mention many God[ly] men who had beards: First, Aaro[n] Moses' brother, definitely had a [ ] beard:

It is like the precious ointment [ ] the head, that ran down upon [ ] beard, even Aaron's beard: tha[t] down to the skirts of his garm[ent] (Psalm 133:2)

We also see that Samson, wh[o] the Nazirite (or Nazarite) vo[w] must have surely had a beard[ ] That he told her all his heart, [ ] said unto her, There hath not [ ] razor upon mine head; for I ha[ve] been a Nazirite unto God from [ ] mother's womb: if I be shaven, th[en] my strength will go from me, and [I] shall become weak, and be like any [ ] other man. (Judges 16:17)

Cont. Pg 3

I was so excited! I began to dream about what I could do to be selected. But the more I thought about it, I couldn't do any of those things.

OH NO!   Was I just an average reindeer?

By the way, who or what was JSN anyway?

For days the announcement was the talk of our village. What would the team do, how was someone selected and who was JSN? No one seemed to have any answers.

Despite everyone's excitement, I became very sad. The little hope I had of being chosen continued to fade away after being around my friends.

They were stronger, smarter and more special than I was. I just knew I'd never be selected for the team.

Then my sadness turned into anger. I wondered what unique skills and an elite team even meant.

The mystery this JSN created no longer interested me. It was probably all a big joke and a waste of my time.

I needed to focus on the important things in my life— like school. Yes, even reindeer go to school.

I enjoyed math and science the most, but my favorite part of the day might be yours, too: recess!

Now earlier I mentioned reindeer games. There are several to choose from, but none are quite like Monopoly. Gee whiz, another reference to the "most famous" reindeer song. Anyway, my favorite game to play was Trinament.

What is Trinament you ask? Well, it is a sport played by three teams on a field. Throughout the field are randomly placed green, blue and red objects that look like ornaments. Your team earns points by placing green ornaments on your side and loses points when blue and red are placed on your side.

About a week after the mysterious JSN announcement, we were playing Trinament, and I thought I saw movement near Avalanche Valley.

Everyone knew to stay away from the valley. At any moment a lot of snow could come crashing down from the nearby mountain and bury everything in its path.

WARNING!!!
Avalanche
Valley

Just don't go there

As I looked closer, I realized it was actually an elf who was getting closer and closer to the edge... and then the elf fell down into the valley!

We needed to do something and quickly!

I asked my friend Davis to come with me and told the rest of my friends to go find help.

As we reached the edge we noticed the elf was not moving. We needed to go down there, but if an avalanche started we would all be in serious trouble.

"Stay here Davis," I said. "I'll be right back."

Before I realized what was happening, I found myself carefully inching down to the bottom of the valley as fast as I could.

As I approached the elf, I noticed he was sitting up, but I knew his leg was probably broken.

Before I could ask if he was okay, I heard a "whumpf" behind me.

There was no time for questions.   We had to get out of there as fast as possible.

I ran with all my might. After what seemed like forever I could almost see the top, but my legs felt like cement and my back was tired from carrying the elf.

The rushing snow must have been at my hooves, but I didn't dare look back. Suddenly there was a rock to jump over and...

Everything went completely black.

After a few moments I tried to move my head and legs, but couldn't. I then began to panic. Were we buried under a ton of snow never to be found?

Did I fail to rescue the elf?

I tried to open my eyes.

As I opened them wider I thought I could see outlines of elves and other reindeer, but how could that be?

An antler began nudging me, and I realized it was Davis. "Get up," he said. "You made it."

I stood up and looked down, but the valley was not the same.
There was snow, boulders, broken trees and absolute destruction where
we had just been. It was a disaster!

What a relief, but where was the elf?

A few feet away the elf lay on a
medical sleigh. As I started to walk
towards him I heard...

"Whoa, whoa, whoa. That was quite a brave thing you just did."

I turned around and there was Saint Nick!

"I'm not sure how many other reindeer would have, or even could have, dashed up the valley to save someone," he continued as he helped me up.

"Most impressive."

And that is when I noticed the three small letters stitched on his mittens:

"In fact," Saint Nick whispered with a wink, "I think that will be your new name from now on... Dasher!"

"Attention everyone," Saint Nick shouted to the gathering crowd. "At this time I would like to introduce today's hero... Dasher!"
And that, my friend, is how I first met (Jolly) Saint Nick and got my name.

Saint Nick then took me home and explained his newspaper article to my parents and me. I wanted to join his team more than ever. My parents said the decision was up to me. I immediately said yes!

That day changed my life forever. Most importantly, it taught me to believe in myself and not compare myself to others.
What about the other reindeer? Well, a few weeks later my best friend Dancer would join me, but you will get to know him next time.

Made in the USA
Lexington, KY
26 March 2018

83 of 100

The PolarPress

ISSUE 1224

Attention Young Reindeer

C0-BEQ-897

ISBN 97819863

90000

9 781986 315555